Carnage

Carnage

Maxime Chattam

Translated from the French
by Gallic Books

Gallic Books
London

First published in France as *Carnages* by Pocket, 2006
Copyright © Maxime Chattam, 2005
English translation copyright © Gallic Books 2012

First published in Great Britain in 2012 by Gallic Books,
59 Ebury Street, London, SW1W 0NZ

A CIP record for this book is available from the British Library
ISBN 978-1-906040-41-3

Typeset in Fournier MT by Gallic Books
Printed and bound by CPI Group (UK) Ltd, Croydon, CR0 4YY

2 4 6 8 10 9 7 5 3 1

Prologue

East Harlem Academy, Harlem, 18 November, 8.28 a.m.

The school resembled a stone monster on its knees, its arms spread out between islands of asphalt and patches of grass. The darkness had not yet lifted so that a yellow glow radiated from its entrails, pools of light showing through the rectangular wounds of its concrete skin.

The building knelt there, behind a flag buffeted by the autumn wind and East 120th Street, with its incessant flow of white and red headlights, like so many blood cells feeding the system of veins. Beyond, the blocked network of major arteries pumped into life, gearing up to start another day.

In the small school yard, figures brushed past each other, laughing as they jostled and shoved, some chattering, some complaining, others not saying anything at all. Their dark outlines hurried into the building's gaping mouth and, as they passed in front of the windows, it was as if the monster were winking at the shadowy sky.

The central hallway slowly filled up with students who would soon disperse to their classrooms to soak up knowledge.

Lisa-Marie tied her hair up with an elastic band while her best friend told her about her evening. Lisa-Marie wasn't really listening; she was focusing on a boy she had had her eye on for weeks and who had just appeared. She had to make a good impression. She immediately adjusted her expression – she knew her face was prettier when she smiled. This week, she was determined to get him to talk to her. It was no good just obsessing about it. *Carpe diem*, like it said in the film.

A little further away, Lucas was sitting on one of the radiators under the bay window. He was tired. His heart had been racing for the last minute or so – maybe that was what tachycardia was? The morning spliff had been too strong, for sure. He nodded to himself as he sat there on his own. He'd put too much in, or else the shit had been poor quality. There was too much tar in it … Yeah, that was it.

I'm baked, he thought, with a grin.

His eyes glazed over as he watched the students file past in a long multicoloured procession.

Mario went down the steps to the corridor that led to

the changing rooms. He hated starting the week with PE – sport was not his thing. He was overweight, which didn't help. He had to get himself excused. The doctor should have excused him ages ago, in fact. Yes, next time he would make sure of it …

The bell rang. It reverberated through every hallway, every staircase, every floor.

In the shadows, a teenager whom several witnesses would later identify as Russell Rod, aged seventeen, pulled his hood up, tugging the strings so that it tightened round his face. He was breathing hard.

He pulled on his leather gloves, which crackled as he spread his fingers. He was filled with a sense of power.

His backpack was open at his feet. But it didn't contain exercise books.

Only a black bar that reflected the corridor lights. Long and rectangular.

The magazine of an Uzi submachine gun.

The boy bent to pick it up.

The weapon rose into the air in the school corridor, almost in slow motion.

The improbability of such an object being in this place gave it a different, almost unreal, appearance. It shone.

It seemed elegant.

The teenager carefully stored some extra magazines in his pockets.

And started walking.

A fat student stood in front of the changing-room door.

The barrel of the Uzi pointed at him.

Lisa-Marie leant against the wall outside the classroom, waiting for the teacher. Just opposite, the boy she fancied was with a group of students who were chatting as they waited. He was Hispanic; she preferred Hispanic guys. And he was really cute.

A series of sharp blasts rang out so loudly that most of the students covered their ears, wincing. Several of them jumped.

They all looked at each other. One of them began to laugh hysterically. The others exchanged glances that were curious, surprised or a bit worried. Some of them were unfazed and resumed their conversations.

Lisa-Marie left the line to go and stand in the middle of the corridor to try to see what was happening. The fire doors were closed. There was nothing to see.

Then one of the doors shook. It began to open. A leg

appeared, then the rest of the body. Holding something strange in its hand ...

Lisa-Marie didn't hear the next shots go off, nor the panicked shrieks of those nearby.

Her head had just exploded.

The boy she had fancied a second earlier was now covered with her brains, splinters of bone and burnt fragments of her long red hair.

Lucas let out a long sigh. The deafening noise was getting closer and boring into his head. What on earth was that racket? Roadworks?

Right now, though, he had something else to worry about.

He was late. And he absolutely had to go to class. He was stoned and if Derringer, his maths teacher, noticed him because he was late he would be in big trouble.

Get up.

He saw a girl he didn't recognise run past him, fast. Lucas frowned.

Then two more ran past.

Then another.

They looked terrified.

What the hell?

Lucas wanted to stand up but couldn't. The state he was in, he'd have to try harder.

That was some shit he'd smoked.

Four more figures ran past him.

The hammering noise started up again. Louder than before.

Lucas put his head in his hands, moaning.

The next moment someone was standing in front of him.

He sat up a little to see who it was.

Did he know him?

There was a strong smell coming from him, pungent.

'What d'you want?' Lucas asked, straining to make out the guy's face.

The other boy raised his arm. There was a gun in his hand. Lucas made a face, wrinkling his nose.

'Oh, man …'

The next second the impact of the bullets flung his body

backwards so violently he ended up embedded in the bay window.

His blood began to flow down the outside of the glass.

A dozen dark-red rivulets dripped to the ground.

And the shots continued to ring out.

8.34 a.m. Fourteen people were dead.

Twenty-one were wounded, some permanently.

Hundreds would be scarred for ever by what they had seen.

Outside, the world was waking up.

To start another day.

1

Lamar Gallineo was nervous.

He was driving his old Pontiac up Third Avenue towards Harlem, and the coffee he had just picked up threatened to spill all over the dashboard.

Lamar was hunched over, too tall to sit comfortably in a normal car. He was slightly over six foot seven.

His height had made it difficult for him to join the police department. Nothing about him was standard, and that was a bad thing.

After studying law, he had wanted to join the NYPD at the highest possible level, as a detective. Which was another bad thing. Since he was black. Or African-American as everyone was supposed to say nowadays.

At the time, the old-timers in the NYPD administration still thought that six-foot-seven black men should be playing basketball, not working as police detectives.

Twelve years on, Lamar carried his badge proudly.

Even better, he worked for the central homicide squad of

the NYPD. A few brilliant flashes of intuition meant that he had been put in charge of several significant cases, which he had solved without making waves. He had rapidly climbed through the ranks. Now he was a lieutenant. The new politics of affirmative action had helped him; he was under no illusion about that. But so much the better, he thought. You had to take your chances where you could find them.

He'd got used to many things over his twelve years. Bad racist jokes from his partners. Long gruelling hours that had destroyed his private life. Decomposing corpses.

But he had never been able to get the hang of driving fast in Manhattan.

His head was bent over the steering wheel in order not to brush against the roof of the car. He was frowning, trying to anticipate the path of the vehicles that might cut him up. The Pontiac's flashing light turned silently, without the siren – Lamar detested the idea of sirens always blaring in the city, saying it put crime and accidents at the forefront of everyone's minds – while he tried to navigate his way through heavy traffic.

He'd been called out on an emergency.

A mass shooting, they'd said.

It was the cops of the 25th precinct who'd contacted him. An unidentified individual had opened fire in the middle of a high school, less than half an hour earlier. Homicide. Harlem. A sensitive situation. This was the kind of tragic scenario that called for Lamar Gallineo.

The sky was barely light when he arrived in front of the school, which was cordoned off with yellow police tape and bathed in the red and blue of the emergency lights. Two police officers immediately came over to meet him as TV vans drew up with a screeching of tyres outside the building.

'Over here, Detective, come inside,' said the first officer, who was squeezed into a uniform that could barely contain his impressive paunch. 'The most seriously injured have been taken away in ambulances, the rest are being treated in the classrooms. We've started taking witness statements.'

'Are you sure the shooter isn't still in there?' demanded Lamar in his deep baritone.

'We know where he is,' replied the second police officer sharply.

Lamar frowned, surprised not to see more activity. If the gunman was still in the building, they would have to organise a complete evacuation, and a SWAT team would first have to seal off all the exits.

'Is that it?' pursued Lamar. 'You know where he is – what does that mean? Is he still here?'

'Yes. We've been told he went into a room on the first floor and didn't come out again.'

'How can you be sure? Is there a camera trained on the door?'

Lamar was hurrying now, more and more anxious at the thought that an armed psychopath might be holed up in a high school still full of students.

'It's a janitor's closet and it only opens from the outside,' explained the officer. 'And witnesses say they saw the shooter go inside. Then it went quiet for a minute or two before the gun was fired again, and then it was over.'

They'd arrived at the school entrance where firefighters and paramedics were going in and out of the swing doors.

'Have you been inside to take a look?' asked Lamar, one hand on the door.

The two officers exchanged a brief embarrassed look. 'No,' replied the man with the large belly. 'We thought we'd better wait for you.'

Lamar pursed his lips. 'I see.'

He reached for his weapon and entered the building. He heard moaning and crying.

There were dozens of figures in the hall, sitting on the floor, lying down or huddled up receiving medical attention or answering the questions of the six or so police officers who had responded to the emergency call.

Lamar made for the large wooden staircase opposite the entrance.

The landing on the way up to the first floor was used for

displaying student notices. A crimson sun about three feet in diameter had exploded over the area. Its core consisted of little particles of molten brain that now stuck to the board, and its rays were made of blood, glistening in the harsh light. The linoleum was also streaked with swirls of blood that stretched towards the stairs where pools stagnated, dripping softly.

A beige blanket covered a body. A hand was sticking out.

A hand with short stubby fingers and several rings. And varnished nails.

Lamar stepped over the body, his Walther P99 at the ready, the two police officers at his heels. They climbed the remaining stairs and found themselves in a long corridor with classrooms leading off it.

There was a lot of blood all over the floor, and panicked teenagers and teachers had skated in it, spreading macabre flower patterns as far as the stairs.

Lamar immediately noticed the three bodies. Two boys and an adult.

Most of their body fluids pooled around them, still warm.

The black man looked at them compassionately without for a moment being distracted from his main objective.

One of the officers crept cautiously towards an unmarked wooden door. He pointed his gun at the lock.

'The janitor assured us that there's no way out,' he murmured. 'There's no door handle on the other side; it's just a closet.'

The two officers took up position on either side of the door.

There was a sweetish odour, a mixture of iron and the smell you get in a butcher's shop – the smell of blood – combined with the sharp whiff of gunshot. How many cartridges must have been fired to make the corridor smell like that? wondered Lamar.

The detective hesitated. He could still call out a SWAT team for backup. He didn't have to go in there all on his own.

Too late.

According to witnesses, the gunman had gone into the cupboard, which had no other exit, and then a shot had rung out. Lamar knew that in these sorts of massacres, the perpetrators almost always turned their guns on themselves. So it all fitted. On the face of it there should be nothing in there but a corpse.

Lamar put one hand on the gold doorknob, training his semi-automatic on the opening. His palm was sweaty. He gripped the weapon so tightly his knuckles showed white.

He tugged the door open, moving aside quickly to avoid presenting too easy a target.

The closet was unlit, but the light from the corridor illuminated it completely.

The smell was nauseating.

Someone in military fatigues and a hooded sweatshirt had collapsed amongst the buckets and pails and cleaning products. A bag full of ammunition lay at his feet, with an Uzi abandoned nearby.

Lamar stepped inside.

The man's head was tipped backwards. Lamar had to go in further to see his face.

He saw a pointed chin, thin lips and the fluffy beginnings of a moustache beneath a large nose.

Then there was a confused mess of meat and splinters of bone amid gaping holes.

He had committed suicide – no doubt about it.

The nauseating odour was even more noticeable now. Lamar instinctively began to look at where he had stepped.

It was shit. It smelt of shit.

He searched the tiny space around him.

A cleaning cart was parked to his left, by a rail of overalls and aprons.

A shoe had been tidied underneath.

Lamar started.

It was a sneaker.

He slowly raised his weapon in front of him.

Then moved forward slowly.

The sneaker jolted.

2

Lamar spread his weight evenly between both legs, ready to react to anything.

'Come out of there slowly,' he said. 'There's no point in hiding.'

When still nothing happened, Lamar took another step forward. One of the police officers came in as well, casting a shadow over the closet. Lamar couldn't see very much any more. With one hand he reached towards the overalls and aprons and pushed them briskly aside to reveal the back wall of the closet. His outstretched right arm held his pistol, ready to spray hell out of its metallic mouth.

A teenager jumped, looking up at him in terror.

He was folded in on himself, trying to take up as little space as possible against the wall. His teeth were chattering.

A huge stain spread across the front of his jeans.

He was trembling.

Lamar realised that the smell of excrement was coming from the boy.

Lamar had set up his base in the janitor's office; the large window looking out onto the hall allowed him to keep an eye on all the comings and goings. The telephone rang incessantly.

So far they had counted fourteen dead and several wounded.

The school principal, Allistair McLogan, a man in his fifties with white hair and a grey moustache, had collapsed into an armchair in the corner of the room. He was rubbing his face and shaking his head.

The gunman had been identified fairly rapidly. First of all by some witnesses who had thought they recognised him, in spite of his hood, as one of the school's students, and then from the corpse, which, despite the absence of the top part of its face, had been compared to the student's photo in the administrative files. There was no doubt who it was.

His name was Russell Rod and he was seventeen.

In less than ten minutes, he had emptied half a dozen Uzi cartridges, about two hundred bullets.

Lamar had gathered together all available depositions and had just finished reading them. Several officers were still in the process of taking statements, but already the essential facts were clear.

Russell Rod must have arrived early. So far no one remembered seeing him before the tragedy, but there was still an enormous number of teenagers to interview. He had gone down to the basement, near the locker rooms, to get ready. That was where he'd started his mad spree.

He'd shot a boy in the corridor, before going upstairs and opening fire in the hall at everyone who moved. Then he'd continued up to the first floor, going into several classrooms where students were taking cover. He'd hunted them down as they sheltered behind the tables and shot them like rabbits, some of them at point-blank range, the barrel almost touching them.

As his weapon was blasting out molten lead, some students had attempted to run away down the corridor. Russell Rod had tried to get as many of them as possible. Not without a certain sadism, according to a maths teacher who had seen it all. He said Russell had aimed for the legs of the fleeing students and then gone and shot them point-blank, if possible in the face.

A massacre.

Russell had done everything to ensure that there would be as few witnesses as possible.

Then he had gone into the janitor's closet. There was a gunshot, then silence. Several seconds had gone by before crying, groans and shouts of pain started up.

Lamar pushed the pile of reports to the side of the desk,

putting a rubber stamp-holder on top of them so that they wouldn't be displaced by a draught, and went next door to the nurse's office.

The youth who had been found in the cupboard, one Chris DeRoy, lay on one of the four beds, wrapped in a silver survival blanket. He was brown-haired and brown-eyed, with freckles and a few spots. He was lying in his own filth, waiting for his parents to come with clean clothes. He was slowly recovering from his terrifying experience.

He had spoken to Lamar, in a very quiet voice. He'd seen Russell come up the stairs holding his submachine gun. He'd also had a clear view of a girl's head exploding. So he'd thrown himself into the walk-in closet and tried to hide in a corner. He'd heard the unrelenting gunshots. Everyone was running around. At first he could hear yelling, but then everyone who wasn't dead and hadn't already fled outside understood that if they wanted to survive they would have to shut up in order not to attract the attention of the madman.

Minutes passed and then the door opened and Russell walked in.

He had recognised him. He was wearing what he always wore: combat trousers and a hooded sweatshirt with the name of a heavy-metal band on it.

Chris had seen him come in. He thought he'd heard him mutter something, but he hadn't been able to make out what. Then Russell had taken his Uzi in one hand and pointed it at his head and fired. Half his head had been blown off and splattered over the opposite wall.

At that moment, the door, which closed automatically, had slammed shut and Chris had waited in the dark until the police arrived.

Lamar came over to his bedside. 'Your parents will be here in a minute. Are ... are you sure you don't want to go to the bathroom and clean yourself up?' He hoped the youth would prefer to be undressed but clean under his survival blanket.

Chris shook his head.

'All right then ...'

Lamar was about to offer him a hot drink when the door opened to reveal a well-coiffed brown-haired middle-aged man, closely shaven and dressed in a three-piece suit. Newton Capparel.

'Lamar!' he exclaimed. 'Give me the low-down; we only have a few minutes before the press conference. They're getting impatient out there.'

Lamar folded his arms across his chest.

'Are you taking over the case?' he asked.

'I prefer to say "coordinating". It's the big cheese who's asked for me.'

Lamar nodded. *Of course.* Capparel was articulate, he knew how to handle journalists and he was more presentable than the hulking Lamar, approaching forty and still wearing an eighties anorak over his enormous shirts. At least today he had spared them his beige and brown striped woolly hat. He had forgotten it in his hurry this morning.

'Lamar,' Capparel went on, 'you'll have to come to the press conference as well, but ... er ... stand a little behind.'

Lamar guessed that he would be there to provide the local colour. He would be the token black face to satisfy political correctness.

'Sure,' he mumbled.

He turned to Chris. 'Hang in there, buddy. Your parents are on their way.'

And then he left with Newton Capparel, who was already running over his spiel for the cameras.

The black mouths of the cameras were poised to swallow whatever they were offered and Lamar retreated into the shadows. He detested these corners of buildings flooded with light for filming, nests of microphones pointed up at your chin. After a few minutes the floodlights began to generate warmth despite the autumn wind ruffling everyone's scarves. The effect was surreal, and Lamar found the whole scene disturbing. It was inappropriate and lacking in respect, he thought, whilst being aware that he was out of step with the modern world and its media needs.

Capparel's 'coordinating' meant that he would benefit from everyone else's work without lifting a finger. He would write the final report and take all the credit. Lamar was used to his methods, common to all the big shots in the NYPD, who had their eye on a political post in the medium or long term.

Shortly before eleven o'clock Lamar left the school to return to Precinct 13 on 21st Street in Lower Manhattan where he worked. He got out of his car and went to buy a cup of coffee before going in. He shared his office with one of the teams from the Manhattan homicide squad. As he went into the large room, he heard two men swapping notes and whispering over the file in front of them. The rest of the chairs were empty except for the one opposite Lamar's. Doris Kennington. She was Lamar's favourite work partner. As tiny as he was tall, she was a slim blonde, a bundle of nerves and muscle, a keen practitioner of combat sports and the only woman Lamar knew who never missed a single episode of *Ultimate Fighting*.

'Aren't you supposed to be working on the massacre in Harlem?' she said in surprise.

'Capparel has stolen the show.'

She raised an eyebrow in a gesture that spoke volumes about what she thought of Capparel.

'Mrs Pathrow called from Bellevue Hospital,' she

reported, consulting her notes. 'Her husband has just died, so the attempted murder charge has been changed to homicide and the DA wants to talk to you about it.'

Lamar nodded. 'Is that it?'

'Yes. Maddox and Rod have gone to the West Side. Someone found a body on an apartment balcony. A good start to the homicide day.'

Lamar quickly checked his emails then grabbed his famous woolly hat and went off to the DA's office.

Doris watched him leave with his apologetic stride, his interminable arms hanging by his slim thighs, his orange anorak in one hand. Lamar was a phenomenon, as singular in appearance as he was sensitive inside. A giant who lived on his own and devoted himself to his investigations. Doris felt a pang to see him leave.

Her eyes went back to the TV, which was silently showing images of the high-school massacre on a loop.

East Harlem Academy was the starting point of a virus.

The source of an epidemic.

Evil was now spreading across the city.

Very soon it would be manifest everywhere.

And would kill, again and again.

Doris leant over and extinguished the tube of doom.

3

'What hope is there for a world in which the young have gone mad?' asked the journalist. The voice crackled in the depths of Lamar's old Pontiac.

Three weeks had gone by since the killings in Harlem.

There had been another massacre at a high school in Queens a few days ago. Twenty-two dead and thirty-one wounded. The crazed gunman, a pupil at the school, had fled after his shoot-out. He had been found at home, having killed himself with a shot to the head.

Neither Lamar nor his closest colleagues had attended – it was outside their jurisdiction. Detectives from Queens had speedily concluded their investigation.

Two teenagers in ten days had opened fire on their schoolmates. The media were obsessed with the story. New Yorkers were beginning to agonise. The entire city trembled in incomprehension.

Lamar contented himself with following the story from afar. As with the Harlem case, no one knew what had motivated the killer. Various psychiatrists were paraded on television to explain that at that age it wasn't necessary to have a clear motive for violence. Persistent emotional disorder coupled with the various violent influences in modern society could culminate in such acts. On other channels, other psychiatrists, equally convinced of their own theories, declared that, on the contrary, the perpetrators would have to have suffered some significant trauma. The experts argued the toss endlessly.

In truth, Lamar concluded, no one knew what caused such things.

What troubled him most was the absence of any leads at all on where the murder weapons had come from. They had nothing to go on in either case. Lamar hoped this would soon change.

He parked in the underground parking garage of the building where he had his meeting and took a lift that smelt of pizza. A bearded man wearing thin glasses and a bow tie greeted him. He was Professor Gavensoort.

'Welcome, Lieutenant,' he said. 'It's always a pleasure to see you here. Newton Capparel sent you, I presume?'

'Yes, I've come about the Uzi that was used in the high-school shooting in Harlem. Apparently you've got some news?'

Gavensoort raised a forefinger. 'Oh, that, yes! Come.'

He strode off down one of the corridors of the NYPD

ballistics lab until he came to a room with white tile flooring, where several firearms were laid out on a lab bench amongst vials and swabs.

'Lieutenant ...?'

'Gallineo.'

'Yes, I remember now, Lieutenant Gallineo. I'm sure you're aware that nowadays criminals try to cover their tracks by filing off the serial numbers of their weapons. That way they hope we won't be able to trace where a particular gun has come from. In fact, for a good few years now forensics have been able to reveal numbers that have been rubbed off. It's not a new technique, but it still works just fine. It's a two-pronged approach, polishing the surface and applying an acid wash.'

'Have you found out where the Uzi came from?'

Seeing that Lamar wanted to get straight to the point, Gavensoort skipped the explanations and got down to the facts.

'No. The serial number was melted off, probably using a blowtorch delicate enough not to have damaged the rest of the weapon. They've gone so deep there's nothing left of the engraving at all.'

Lamar scratched his chin.

'Would you need specialist tools for that?'

'Not really. Plumbers, firefighters, mechanics … all kinds of people use that sort of thing.'

'I can't imagine the gunman, a seventeen-year-old kid, going to that amount of trouble to get rid of a serial number.'

'Gangs can usually organise it if they know what they're doing,' countered the professor.

'From what I've been told, Russell wasn't exactly a model student, but he wasn't part of a gang either.'

Gavensoort shrugged his shoulders.

'Well, that's up to you to work out – my job's just to look at the technical side of things. But I've got something else you might find interesting,' he added without pausing for breath, pointing to two pistols.

As far as Lamar remembered, no other weapons had been found at the scene at the high school or even at Russell Rod's home.

'These two semi-automatics were used in the Queens high-school shooting last week. I was brought in on that one too.'

'And?'

Gavensoort stared back at the detective, drawing out the suspense.

'The serial numbers were erased in exactly the same way as with the Uzi,' he eventually explained. 'So there's a link between the two attacks. As to who and why, well, that's your ball game. My report's on the table in the lobby. I'm sending a copy to the Queens detectives.'

Lamar was standing open-mouthed when his cell rang. Doris's piercing voice came down the line.

'Lamar, you need to get over to the Lower East Side right now.'

There was panic in her voice.

'Why? What is it, Doris? You sound—'

'There's been another shooting, at a high school …'

The school was very close to the Williamsburg Bridge, a neighbourhood that roared with continual traffic noise. Three police cars had pulled up outside the main entrance, their lights still flashing, and a uniformed officer was sealing off the area with yellow and black tape.

Lamar walked into the entrance hall, strangely similar to the one at the school in Harlem, and was met by wailing and tears. First-aiders moved busily amongst lifeless bodies, their feet slipping in pools of blood. Dozens of red footprints zigzagged across the floor.

Lamar stopped an officer passing within earshot.

'Lieutenant Gallineo,' he announced. 'What do we know about the gunman? Still here?'

The officer, a Hispanic woman, shook her head.

'No, witnesses say they saw him go out the back, toward the little park. We've got cars out looking for him. He's been described as medium build, wearing blue jeans and a hooded black parka. Nothing more at the moment.'

Lamar thanked her. As he wrote these meagre facts down in his notebook, Doris appeared at his side, eyes wide and darting around the room.

'Doris, can you start gathering information? I'm going to look for the gunman – he could still be in the area.'

She gave a quick nod and Lamar bounded off down a long corridor, at the end of which he found the back entrance to the school.

A park made up of narrow paths and scrawny shrubs ran along the other side of the road, surrounded by grey and brown tenement buildings.

Lamar headed down the nearest path and took out his gun. This was the part of his job he least enjoyed. Hunting down a suspect. Maybe because his size made him an easy target he'd never felt comfortable in pursuit. Observation, interrogation and deduction suited him much better.

Holding his Walther P99 against his thigh, Lamar continued along damp pathways, passing a bench and a fountain before coming to a crossroads from which several routes led further into the park. Although the park wasn't very big, there were several entrances and the gunman could easily have escaped by now. Lamar let himself relax slightly.

Now's not the time to lose focus!

That was how accidents happened.

He decided to take the path on the left, but changed his mind when he saw something shimmering on the lawn in front of him. As he got closer, he saw that it was a shiny cartridge. He was about to lean forward to get a better look, but stopped himself at the last moment. He gripped his gun tightly. He was already squatting and, without standing up straight again, scanned his surroundings.

He had the feeling he was being watched.

Fear breeds fear …

It was enough to have the sensation of being watched to convince yourself it was actually happening; your imagination played tricks on you. He had to force himself to concentrate.

There were several clumps of thick shrubs around him, one larger than the rest, and a little bit nearer. Lamar stood up and stepped very slowly towards it, his finger ready to pull the trigger. The shrubbery was neatly trimmed into a U shape with the opening to the side. Lamar moved closer and closer, but still couldn't see inside.

A dark patch began to emerge through the branches and the few leaves that were still on the plants. There was something in there.

Lamar held the Walther P99 out in front of him.

With a quick sidestep, he faced the opening head-on, primed to dive in and shoot.

The thicket was shaped like this in order to allow workmen access to maintenance tunnels. The dark patch Lamar had seen was a water point, probably used by the gardeners. Next to it was a steel double trapdoor. A tiny sign forbade unauthorised entry.

Lamar took a small torch from the pocket of his shapeless anorak, tucking it under the arm holding the gun before lifting the trapdoor with his other hand.

There was a ladder leading down several feet into the total darkness.

Lamar clenched his teeth. He couldn't stand situations like this.

But, even if he called for backup, someone would still have to be the first to go down. Lamar bent down to shine the light around. Nothing jumped out at him. He wedged the torch between his teeth and ventured down the metal rungs. With each step, he sank further into the city's underbelly.

He was breathing heavily as his foot touched the ground.

He'd made it down; no shots had greeted his arrival. Still, he circled round, making sure there was no immediate danger.

Pipes and knobs of all shapes and sizes jutted out from the floor and walls, climbing up towards the surface. In another part of the wall, there was a door with a chain and an old broken padlock across it. And then Lamar found the shooter.

He was right there.

Right in front of him.

Watching him without batting an eyelid. His weapon gleaming in the faint torchlight.

4

Lamar emerged from the underground room, breathing out heavily.

He took out his cell phone and called Doris.

'I found him,' he said as soon as she picked up. 'He's put a bullet through his chin. His brain's stuck to the ceiling.'

A few minutes later, the park had been cordoned off and the forensics team was bringing the corpse up in a black body bag.

Lamar found Doris standing to one side, away from the scrum of ambulances and journalists.

'What have you got?' he asked.

'Nothing concrete yet, just a kid who says it might be a guy named Mike Simmons. He recognised what the gunman was wearing, especially the black parka. But he couldn't formally identify him.'

Lamar rubbed his face vigorously with his huge hands.

'What's going on, Lamar? Three high schools in three weeks. Three kids losing it, mowing down their classmates and then putting a bullet through their own brain. Don't you find that alarming? Why do you think it is? Too many video games?'

'No,' he said, without explanation.

Doris held her notebook and pen in front of her. Her blonde fringe was blowing about in the wind. Lamar noticed she had eye make-up on, but her lipstick had worn off. She was so little. Tiny.

'Well, what then?' she pressed him.

Lamar fixed his dark eyes on his partner.

'I think there's a link between all these kids. Between the killers, I mean.'

Doris frowned.

'Before I came back up, I checked out the weapon the kid used,' he said, looking over at the body bag. 'The serial number has been removed in exactly the same way as in the other attacks.'

'Lamar, you shouldn't have touched—'

'Yeah, yeah. Anyway, I'm telling you we won't find any more on that one than we have on the others.'

He bit his lip nervously.

'Something doesn't add up,' he said after a pause.

'What are you thinking? That these three guys knew each other?'

'I don't know yet; we'll have to work that out. All I know is, if it carries on like this, we've got less than a week before the next massacre.'

Before he walked away, Doris placed her hand on her colleague's sleeve.

'But you don't think this is … some kind of epidemic.'

'That's not what I'd call it. But what scares me is this might not be the end of it.'

'But how can it carry on? I mean, they're killing themselves every time.'

'It's just a feeling I've got. Now, I'd like you to carry out some enquiries here. Can you ask the students if they knew about this underground room? Push them a bit; I want them to talk.'

'And what'll you do?'

'Try to understand. Try to see how three teenagers without a record, without any real history of troublemaking, could get hold of weapons which all seem to have passed through the same hands. Before going out and gunning down their buddies on a clear fall morning.'

Lamar started his Pontiac, his cell phone wedged between his ear and shoulder.

'Doug, could you do something for me?' he asked. 'Get me the names of everyone who's known for handling firearms, fixing them up, selling them on, everything you've got. Call the Firearms Department if you need to. And if you find anyone with a background of mental health problems, would you put those on the top of the pile? I'll owe you, Doug.'

Douglas's gravelly voice came back down the line, made hoarse by the cigarette smoke that permanently wreathed his lips.

'This for the high-school shooting? You got a lead?'

'Until we have one, I want to be sure we've gone down every possible route. Let's keep in touch.'

Lamar hung up and turned down Clinton Street. Doris's idea of some kind of teen epidemic of murderous madness seemed out of the question. There was no rational basis for it.

Yet the short space of time between each attack, the clean records of all the perpetrators and the similarities in the weapons used did suggest a possible link. The idea of a connection was daring, certainly, but not outlandish.

Someone was working in the background. Someone

who could get hold of an untraceable gun. Someone with a knack for manipulating impressionable boys.

Lamar's first instinct had been to think of a youth worker, or a teacher. Someone in regular contact with teenagers, who knew how to talk to them and take them under their wing. But now he wasn't so sure. Convincing a teenage boy to open fire on his classmates before turning the gun on himself was a seriously twisted act – and not easy to accomplish. It would have to be someone with extraordinary powers of persuasion and charisma, willing to use whatever methods were necessary. In short, this person had to be one of a kind. Who could have pulled it off? Three times in a row!

Maybe Lamar's theory didn't stand up after all. But he couldn't quite brush it aside. There had to be a link between these three suicidal kids. Just the guns, all made unidentifiable in the same way, were proof enough. That couldn't possibly be a coincidence.

Lamar knew that real life was a long way from fiction or TV shows. Most people didn't go to that much trouble to cover up their crimes. Very few of them knew that the police could glean a mass of information from a firearm and that it could lead them back to its last owner. A firearm is made and registered under its serial number and, when it's sold, its owner becomes associated with that number. If this person sells it on, the new owner is in turn put on file, and so on. In the majority of cases, once the weapon is found, it leads straight to its owner. If it wasn't the owner who committed the crime, if he lent the gun to someone or sold it on illegally, rigorous questioning will usually dig up enough information to work out who had it last.

The most seasoned, well-organised criminals have seen all these police techniques before. Consequently, they buy their guns legitimately – contrary to popular belief, it's easy to buy a gun in the USA but less easy to get your hands on one illegally, and, if you do, there's always the chance you'll get shopped for it – and try to get rid of the serial number by filing or hammering it off. But forensic techniques can usually uncover traces of the engraving and reveal the precious number.

All this helped Lamar to make one significant deduction: the man or woman who had supplied the guns to the youngsters was a real veteran of crime who'd seen it all and kept their hand in. There was no doubt they would be known to the police, probably for trafficking firearms.

The name of this person must be buried somewhere in the police files – the person responsible for this carnage, or the person who could at least lead Lamar to whoever was responsible.

Lamar came back onto First Avenue and passed the UN tower, heading north towards Harlem.

He got his phone out again to call Professor Gavensoort.

'Professor,' he began, 'it's Lieutenant Gallineo. I wanted to ask you something. There were fingerprints on the weapon. Did you manage to lift them off?'

'Yes, Lieutenant. Nothing out of the ordinary there; in both cases the fingerprints were those of the gunman. Which you'd know already if you'd looked at my report.'

'Thank you. Just wanted to check.'

He hung up abruptly to spare himself further comment from the professor.

They had nothing to go on.

Three killers who'd killed themselves.

And a link between them: their weapons.

Lamar gripped the steering wheel.

They had to act quickly – he knew it.

They had to find a lead and work out what was really going on in the background, behind these child assassins.

Because Lamar was willing to bet things were not at all as they seemed.

A dark secret hovered in the shadows.

5

East Harlem Academy had reopened its doors, the yard and lino floors of the crime scene once again trampled under its students' feet. Walking towards the entrance during the lunch break, Lamar was surprised to see smiles and laughter on these young faces. In adolescence, every day is a new dawn, not connected to what's gone before. It occurred to Lamar that in adulthood we look back over our lives as a timeline punctuated with big events, whereas in childhood time is grasped in fragments, compartmentalised. It was making this transition that brought you to the age of reason.

Lamar veered off to the right in the hallway, towards the janitor's room. A tall, gruff man in his forties, the janitor's hair was cut so short he looked bald from a distance. Lamar had noticed this the first time he'd seen him, barely three weeks earlier. The janitor stood up so straight you'd think he'd just come out of the army.

'Hello …'

Lamar wagged his finger and screwed up his eyes while trying to remember his name.

'Quincey. Frank Quincey. What can I do for you, Detective?'

'Do you know the kids pretty well? You're here all the time …'

Quincey pulled a face.

'Well, I guess I end up knowing more or less which one's which. Why d'you ask?'

'Russell Rod, the gunman. Know which one he was?'

'Oh, him, yeah. Seemed nice enough. You know, they're not bad kids here. Lots of 'em come to see me when they're bored during recess. Don't tell Principal McLogan, but every now and again they ask me for a cigarette. I try not to give them any, but when they're really polite it's hard to say no.'

'How d'you mean, "really polite"?'

'Oh, you know, they take time to chat, say hi when they walk past. A lot of people just see the janitor as the guy in the blue coat who keeps the building nice, like some kind of ghost. But some of them are really good kids. They even get me chocolates at Christmas!'

'And what about Russell?'

'Well, he kept himself to himself. Didn't pick fights. Always wore heavy-metal-band T-shirts, with camouflage pants. Tell the truth, I don't really know what he got up to

– he wasn't the type to hang out in groups, preferred being on his own. But he never gave me any trouble. No scuffles, no graffiti, none of that stuff.'

Lamar scratched his chin, thinking. What he knew of teen killers fitted pretty well with this picture. Loners, often with no history of trouble. They build up steam like a pressure cooker, and then they explode.

'Didn't he have any friends here?' the lieutenant continued.

'Not that I know of, but then I'm not watching them the whole goddamn day! I only noticed Russell because he often used to sit on his own with his headphones on. I even went over to speak to him a few times, but he wasn't much of a talker.'

A shadow appeared on the floor of the little room.

Allistair McLogan was standing in the doorway.

'Detective?' he said with surprise. 'What are you doing here?'

Lamar raised his eyebrows.

'My job.'

'Yes, I can see that. Well, from now on, I'd appreciate it if you'd stop by my office before interrogating my staff.'

Lamar bristled, more annoyed by the principal's

haughty tone than his throwing his weight around.

'And why's that? Do you need to "brief" the whole place before I get here?'

McLogan shook his head fiercely.

'Of course not, but I do like to know what's going on under my roof. So, have you made any progress with the investigation?'

Lamar dodged the question. 'It's coming along. Since I've got you here, what can you tell me about Russell Rod?'

McLogan's grey moustache twitched.

'Nothing more than I've already told you. A well-behaved boy. Very rarely in my office and never for anything serious. I'll say it again: there was nothing unbalanced about Russell Rod. No one could have predicted what happened. Have you spoken to his parents?'

'A colleague of mine has.'

'Well, perhaps you'd better go see them yourself. They'll tell you the same thing: a perfectly normal kid. I don't know what got into him.'

Lamar took a business card out of his wallet and put it down on Quincey's desk.

'If you think of anything at all ...' he added.

The principal wanted to see him out, but Lamar declined with a determined smile. As he walked back to his car, the air was getting icier. It wouldn't be long before the first snow fell.

Lamar had to admit he wasn't keen on this McLogan. The distraught white-haired man of the day of the massacre had given way to an inquisitor who wanted to rule his school as if it were his kingdom. But he was only trying to protect himself, concluded the lieutenant, which was entirely understandable. The media had laid into him as 'the principal who hadn't seen the threat coming'.

Lamar went back to his office to pore through the files on illegal arms dealers that had been put aside for him.

Since criminal cases were now all logged digitally, he could easily get hold of more detailed reports. He looked into the methods used by the best-known dealers in stolen goods. The first few hours of reading drew a blank.

Late in the afternoon, a note from the Firearms Department came in. It listed a dozen names of individuals known to have used a blowtorch to remove serial numbers from firearms.

Lamar spent the next three hours 'placing' these suspects.

Six of them were still in prison. Four had no permanent residence and of the last two, one had been dead a year and a half, and the other had left the state for Florida six months earlier.

Lamar let out a long sigh.

He went home around ten for a night of dreamless sleep, and was one of the first back in the office the next day. He caught up with Capparel in the late morning. The three suicides had been confirmed. Detectives had interviewed the parents, blended families or single mothers in all three cases. They had turned the kids' bedrooms upside down.

There was no link.

Lamar pressed Capparel on the similarities in the weapons used, adamant it was too much of a coincidence to be just that. Capparel paused for a moment, before giving Lamar the go-ahead to dig deeper in that direction.

The giant, as his partners called him, was heading out for lunch when he passed Doris in the corridor.

'Oh good, I was looking for you,' she said. 'I'm going to give this to Capparel. I've made you a copy. It's my report on the students I spoke to yesterday.'

'So what came out of it?'

'Not much, although a lot of them knew about that underground room. They hid down there to smoke – marijuana, most likely. The gunman's body has been identified, and it's who we thought, Michael Simmons. One of the kids recognised him by what he was wearing.'

'Anything else?'

'That's all for now.'

Lamar nodded gloomily. Things were not moving along as quickly as he would have liked.

Doris invited him to join her for lunch, and the two of them went down to eat a bowl of pasta at the little restaurant across the road. Lamar talked about the investigation. Doris talked about her date the previous night. Each was engrossed in their own subject.

They left the restaurant at around one o'clock. Lamar was about to cross the road when his cell phone rang. It was Gavensoort.

'Lieutenant, I've got something for you.'

'What is it?'

'Come right away – this is big.'

'Well, tell me then!'

'I'm telling you, come over here and I'll show you. I think you'll be pleased ...'

Lamar hung up, shaking his head.

The first snowflakes began to fall.

6

The snow had been falling for ten minutes, getting steadily heavier. Huge flakes filled the Manhattan skyline.

Lamar Gallineo's car cleared a path through the fleecy white curtain, before slipping into the underground parking garage of an enormous building.

The lieutenant made his way upstairs, where he was met by Professor Gavensoort, wearing another of the bow ties from his legendary collection.

Without any preamble, Gavensoort tugged Lamar's sleeve and led him through a maze of corridors to a door covered in danger signs and notices warning that 'Unauthorised entry is forbidden'. Opening it, they entered a pristine shooting gallery. Gavensoort disappeared into the adjoining gun room and emerged carrying a Desert Eagle. He handed the hefty pistol to Lamar.

'There you go, Lieutenant.'

'Um, what—'

'Go ahead, take it. Be careful, though, it's loaded.'

Lamar did as he was asked, taking the gun in his hands, while Gavensoort went in search of ear protectors and safety goggles.

'I want you to fire a few bullets at the target back there,' Gavensoort instructed, putting his ear protectors on.

Lamar gave up trying to fathom what was going on. He adjusted his ear protectors and got in position. He had never fired a weapon as powerful as this before. He pulled the trigger.

The gun lifted up in his hand, spitting out a spray of fire and making an unholy racket. Lamar could feel the impact of the shot right up to his shoulder. His ears were ringing even with the ear protectors.

He hadn't hit the target, though it was only thirty feet away. He tried again.

Four more bullets spewed from the barrel.

Three hit the white cardboard, two of them in the stomach of the imaginary assailant. Lamar had done better than usual, and he knew he'd been lucky.

Lamar only realised Gavensoort was clapping when he turned round to return the weapon.

'Not bad!' the professor joked. 'So, what do you make of the Desert Eagle?'

'It's pretty powerful.'

Gavensoort pointed his finger straight at the detective.

'Exactly! Just pulling once on the trigger has a huge impact, doesn't it?'

Lamar nodded.

'Come with me.'

Gavensoort led him into his office, two doors down the hall. He pointed out a little plastic box on his desk.

Lamar picked it up to inspect its contents. Inside was a tiny scrunched-up piece of fabric, no bigger than the nib of a pen.

'I found that caught in the trigger slot.'

'Of which gun?' asked the detective.

'The Desert Eagle used in yesterday's massacre.'

'So have you worked out what it is?'

Gavensoort stroked his beard, a fixed grin on his face.

'It's treated leather. From a glove.'

Lamar frowned.

'A glove?' he repeated.

'That's right. The reason I got you to try out one of our guns was so you could feel for yourself how powerful that Desert Eagle is. That piece of glove leather wouldn't have stayed put if it had been fired again. It must have been torn off when the trigger went back into position. If the trigger had been pulled another time, the leather would have fallen out. But it didn't, because I found it.'

'Which means what? It wasn't used again after it was fired. So what?'

When he wasn't quite following his colleagues' science, Lamar made himself out to be slower than he really was in order to get them to elucidate.

'Come on, Lieutenant! What this clearly means is that the last person to pull the trigger was wearing gloves.'

Lamar nodded. It seemed logical.

'I finally got my hands on the forensic report late this morning. It came with a sealed packet, containing the bullet that went through the head of the "suicide victim". I examined it myself. It's a .44 Magnum. Which matches the Desert Eagle found in the gunman's hand.'

'Mike Simmons. His name was Mike Simmons. So that confirms it was suicide, then.'

'That's not what I said. Pay attention. There are two things you need to be aware of, Lieutenant. Firstly, that the Desert Eagle usually takes a .357 Magnum – the .44 is far less common. Even without having compared the gun barrel with the bullet, I can say with some certainty that it was indeed the weapon used to fire through the young man's skull.'

'And the other thing?'

'The other thing is that according to the forensic report – and you'll be able to confirm this, since you were at the scene – Mike Simmons was not wearing gloves. What do you make of that?'

Lamar was growing tense.

'Did you get any fingerprints off the Desert Eagle?'

'I had to wait a while for forensics before I could compare. They're the right ones. What I mean is, it's Mike Simmons's prints on the gun.'

Lamar stepped back until he was perching on a corner of the desk.

Mike Simmons had gone down into that dark room with the Desert Eagle, turned it on himself and fired, with his bare hands. But the clue that had been found inside the weapon proved that the last person to fire the semi-automatic was wearing leather gloves ...

'So, how do you explain that?' pressed Gavensoort.

'I'm not sure yet,' mumbled Lamar, standing up straight. Then he added more confidently, 'But I'll get there.'

By the time Lamar Gallineo was back at the wheel of his car, everything was covered in a thick white blanket, and it was even harder to see where he was going. At this rate, it would soon be impossible to see across the street.

He pressed 2 on his cell phone and Doris's number was dialled automatically.

'Doris, it's Lamar,' he said. 'Tell me something. When you were taking statements from the students yesterday, did they say anything about what Mike Simmons was wearing?'

'Not really. I don't think they were paying much attention to that. They were so freaked out by what was going on.'

'Did anyone mention gloves? Was Simmons wearing gloves?'

'I have no idea. You know, most of those kids were in shock. They didn't even know who was shooting at them until he was named on TV!'

'Really?'

'Yeah, well, everything was happening so fast they couldn't really tell. All they knew was that one of their classmates had turned up and started firing at them, so they panicked, obviously. In the end, we figured out his name after two boys recognised him by his big black parka. But, you know, in these situations everyone's just trying to get away from the gunman, so they're not exactly picking up on the little details! So if you want to find out if Simmons was wearing gloves you'd better talk to forensics.'

The line was breaking up and he was struggling to hear Doris's voice.

'I've already read their report. It's the eye-witness statements I'm interested in.'

'I put a copy of my report on your desk at lunchtime. It's all in there.'

He thanked her and hung up before they were cut off.

The whole business was getting stranger by the minute. He would need to go right back to the beginning and look at everything again.

Anxious to get back to base, Lamar drove as fast as he safely could in the frozen conditions. Cars were crawling along with their headlights on.

New York was being buried deeper and deeper under a thick coat of white powder.

When Lamar arrived back at his desk with two warm cups of coffee, Doris was nowhere to be seen. He sat down and piled up all the paperwork in front of him. He separated out the toxicology and ballistics reports, the forensic findings and statements from all the police officers who had been at the scene.

Lamar began with the ballistics report from the first massacre. Various comparisons had been made and notes taken about calibres of weapons, but nothing stood out.

With Gavensoort's words ringing in his ears, Lamar went on to the files relating to the crime scene at the park, where the body of the third suicide victim, Mike Simmons, had been found. No gloves had been picked up from the surrounding area.

Lamar flicked through the forensic report on Mike Simmons. The list of belongings found on his person included his clothing and the contents of his pockets. One detail in particular caught Lamar's eye.

There was a pair of gloves. Woollen gloves. *Woollen!* The glove that had been caught in the Desert Eagle's trigger was made of leather.

Something wasn't right. Things were not as they seemed, Lamar was sure of it. He needed to pin down what else didn't fit so that he could find a *real* lead to follow up.

He went back over the eye-witness statements from the high school in Harlem. Nothing.

Doris's report. The kids had all panicked. Nothing in particular had stood out to them. No one had mentioned any gloves. Nor had they said they definitely hadn't seen gloves on the gunman's hands. Lamar sat back in his chair. It was cold, so most of the kids would have been wearing gloves.

As Doris had said, many of the students hadn't had any idea who was firing on them. Some described him as 'a guy running really fast', or 'a dark shadow chasing around the school'. Several witnesses had confirmed that Simmons had pulled up his hood, making him an even more intimidating sight during the shootings. A faceless, anonymous being. The grim reaper, holding a gun where his scythe should have been.

Lamar rested his chin on his hand. He went back over his files. He found the bundle of witness statements from the East Harlem Academy students. After several minutes of studying the same pages for the umpteenth time, he finally found what he was looking for.

It was a description of the gunman, Russell Rod. He had been wearing a hood, pulled down over his face.

At the back of his desk, Lamar dug out a copy of the Queens investigation. He went over the witness statements.

Again, the gunman had been wearing a hood. The three boys had all used weapons from the same source. None of them had been in trouble before. They'd each fired on their classmates one morning, three teenagers in the space of three weeks. And they all wore hoods to disguise themselves, to look more mysterious, more frightening.

This couldn't just be a coincidence. Someone was pulling the strings, manipulating these boys.

Lamar rubbed his temples. He couldn't make sense of it

all. Who could have had such an influence over these three quiet kids? They were all the same type: loners. Which made them easier targets.

Who was it? Lamar clenched his fist. *Who was it?*

He skimmed over his notes one last time. It was all becoming a blur.

Names and ages of witnesses, their statements inside quotation marks.

Lamar could see some of their faces.

Their words were spread out in front of him.

Then he remembered arriving at the scene of the first attack.

The voices, shouting over one another, wailing. The other cops there with him.

The initial run-down of what had happened.

Voices … Lamar could still hear them all. Words …

A police officer telling him, 'And witnesses say they saw the gunman go inside. Then it went quiet for a minute or two before the gun was fired again, and then it was over.'

He leapt up, grabbed his anorak and hurried down the corridor.

7

It was mid afternoon when Lamar walked into the hall of East Harlem Academy and headed towards the janitor's room.

Frank Quincey was inside, fixing a broken desk lamp.

'Lieutenant … any news?'

'I need some information on a student.'

Quincey tilted his head back.

'Ah, well, you'd better talk to McLogan about that, hadn't you?'

'I'd rather avoid the principal, actually. We don't exactly see eye to eye.'

Quincey made a face.

'Hmm, could be tricky. What is it you're after?'

'I need to see one of the kids' files.'

Running his fingers through his close-cropped hair, Quincey thought for a minute.

'OK, there might be a way. Come with me.'

They walked through the building and entered an office off the library. A slightly plump woman was typing at her computer.

'Leslee, could you help us a second? The detective needs to take a look at something.'

Leslee looked up until finally her eyes alighted on the face of the man towering in front of her.

'We need access to a student file right away,' said Lamar.

'You'll need to see Mr McLogan about—'

'He's busy right now,' he cut in, 'and it can't wait.'

She shook her head to show she wasn't happy with the idea, but Lamar could tell it was just for form's sake.

'So what's this kid's name?' she asked in her shrill voice.

'Chris DeRoy – probably Christopher, I guess.'

'DeRoy,' she echoed, typing in the name. 'Just a moment …'

Lamar's cell phone rang. Doris's name flashed up on the screen.

'Lamar, is everything OK? I heard you ran out of the office.'

'Yeah, I'm at the high school in Harlem, checking something out.'

'Oh yeah? What is it?'

Lamar stepped out of the office and into the empty library so that he could talk freely without being overheard.

'Something's bugging me,' he said mysteriously.

'Well, go on, what?'

Lamar took a deep breath, then launched in.

'Something I remembered. When I arrived at the scene of the crime, the cops told me the killer was still there. Witnesses said he walked into a closet that could only be opened from outside. A couple of minutes went by before they heard a shot.'

'OK ... makes sense so far. After what he'd just done, Russell Rod probably needed a moment to get his head straight ... before putting a gun to it.'

'Except that we have a witness to the suicide, Chris DeRoy. He was so scared he shit himself. And he saw Russell shoot himself before the door closed!'

'So?'

'So the door didn't take a couple of minutes to shut! It doesn't add up. Either the witnesses got it wrong and there were only ten or so seconds before the gunshot, or else ... DeRoy's lying.'

Through the window, the detective saw the principal charging towards him, on the warpath.

'Lamar, I wouldn't waste too much time over this,' warned Doris. 'In these kinds of traumatic events, our concept of time goes out the window. People get totally muddled—'

Lamar jumped in.

'Not to the point of confusing ten seconds with two minutes!'

Quincey appeared in the doorway.

'We've got something,' he whispered.

'Gotta go,' he told Doris, hanging up.

He hurried into the office.

'Bingo! I've got a Christian DeRoy,' announced Leslee.

'That'll be him,' Lamar confirmed.

'What is it you want to know?'

Lamar nudged closer to get a better look at the screen, which seemed to make Leslee uneasy.

The door was flung open and McLogan stormed in.

'What the hell's going on here, Lieutenant? I quite clearly told you that if you needed anything at all you were to come to me!'

Lamar took his badge from his pocket.

'See this? What this means is we both have a job to do. My job is to lead my inquiry the way I see fit. And yours, sir, is to leave me the hell alone so I can concentrate on arresting those responsible for this massacre.'

McLogan's face flushed bright red, in stark contrast to his white hair and grey moustache.

'Don't you dare talk to me like that!' he shouted. 'The person responsible for this killed himself! You have no reason to be here.'

Lamar leant towards Leslee.

'I need to know what class he's in and where I can find him right now. Plus his address, while we're at it.'

Leslee looked wide-eyed back at him.

'But, um ... I ... er ...'

'You don't want to be getting into trouble with the police now, do you, Leslee?' Lamar warned sternly.

She gulped, her eyes flicking to and fro between Lamar and a seething McLogan.

'May I remind you that fourteen people are dead,' Lamar added, sticking the knife in.

He could see the librarian's eyes welling up.

Leslee clicked open a folder entitled 'Personal details'.

'Here's his address. 122nd Street, just around the corner.'

Lamar made a note of it and was about to point to the 'Student grade and assessments' tab when something stopped him.

The details underneath the heading 'School record' caused a shiver to run down his spine.

Christian DeRoy had been to five different schools over the last few years, expelled from each of them for bad behaviour.

The first high school on the list was the scene of the Queens attack.

'Scroll down a bit, would you?' he asked.

The next was the school by the Williamsburg Bridge.

'Is something wrong, Detective?' Quincey asked anxiously, seeing the troubled look on Lamar's face.

Lamar pointed at the screen.

'Which class is Chris DeRoy in right now?'

McLogan sighed loudly. 'Your superiors are going to hear about this!' he threatened.

Leslee scanned through the file to find the student's

schedule. She opened her mouth to give the room number, but then froze.

'What is it?'

'Um, well, he's not in class. We got a letter from a psychologist who's been treating him since ... since the tragedy three weeks ago,' she read out, placing her hand against her heart. 'Christian DeRoy is suffering from post-traumatic stress disorder and is still not well enough to attend classes.'

She lifted her eyes from the screen when she heard a commotion, turning round in time to see the detective's back as he sped out of the room.

Lamar had broken into a sprint.

8

The Pontiac skidded about in the snow, the back of the vehicle slewing across the road, forcing Lamar to slow right down in order to regain control of the car.

Snowflakes continued to fall by the million.

The roads were by now entirely fleece-lined and every building wore a white cap.

Lamar called Doris back.

'Doris, I need your help,' he said, trying to keep his voice steady. 'Meet me at 158 East 122nd Street, quick as you can. I think I've found our man.'

'Huh? What are you saying?'

'The kid who was in the closet with Russell Rod. It's him, Doris.'

'Him what? Calm down and tell me what's going on.'

'He lied. He said he saw Russell Rod come in and shoot himself just before the door swung shut. It's not true. DeRoy is a troubled kid, he's been to five different schools and been expelled from all of them. And three of those schools are where the attacks have taken place! It was him – he was the gunman every time! Russell Rod, the boy from Queens and Mike Simmons, all of them were victims, not the killers!'

'What? You mean he was the one ... But how?'

'The hood, Doris! All three gunmen were wearing hoods to hide their faces. The handful of witnesses who thought they recognised them based it on their clothes every time. But it was DeRoy wearing their clothes! That's why the supposed gunmen shot themselves out of view of everyone else.'

Lamar braked suddenly, spotting a red light at the last minute. The Pontiac skidded off course again, sliding into the middle of the intersection. Two vans started honking their horns. Lamar carried on explaining his theory, while slowly reversing back behind the line.

'Chris DeRoy may be crazy, but he's smart too. He played the victim so he could mow down his classmates and teachers, then he snuck off to where the guy whose identity he'd stolen was waiting for him. They changed clothes, and then he shot him through the head.'

'I guess that makes sense ...'

'Of course it does! The first time, at the Harlem high school, he arrived early in the morning with Russell Rod. He made him go into the closet while he went around shooting at everybody, wearing Russell's clothes. When he was done, he went back into the closet and swapped the clothes back, which is why it was a couple of minutes before the gun went off.'

'Machiavellian …'

'Doris, come meet me as quick as you can. I don't want to call the local cops. You never know how a kid like DeRoy might react if he sees a heap of police cars screeching up to his door.'

'I'm on my way, Lamar.'

The windscreen wipers cleared the layer of snow that was slowly building up on the Pontiac's windscreen. For ten minutes, Lamar had been sitting outside the three-storey building where Chris DeRoy and his parents lived.

Doris walked along the pavement towards him, accompanied by a stocky Puerto Rican-looking man sporting a bushy moustache. Lamar got out of the car to meet them.

'D'Amato was twiddling his thumbs so I brought him along,' explained Doris.

'It's the house across the road there. Doris, come with me, we'll take the front door. D'Amato, you go round the back, in case he tries to get out that way. We'll give you a couple of minutes to get in position.'

D'Amato nodded and jogged away, leaving deep

footprints along the snow-covered pavement.

While they waited, Doris tried to pick holes in her colleague's line of argument, though she had to admit it was pretty convincing.

'How could Chris DeRoy have gotten Russell Rod to come to school early and follow him into this closet then later gotten Mike Simmons to follow him down to that underground room?'

'He could have told them anything. That he had a surprise for them, or wanted them in on a joke or some trick he was going to play – who knows?'

'But nothing came up in the toxicology reports, so he can't have drugged them to get them to stay put while he went out shooting his classmates. There were no marks found on their wrists to indicate they'd been tied up either.'

Lamar stared back at his partner. He put two fingers together in the shape of a gun and mimed shooting himself in the head. He'd thought of everything. And for every question he'd asked himself, he'd come up with a logical answer.

'First off he hit them over the head to knock them out,' he replied. 'Then he took off wearing their clothes and went on a killing spree. He picked these guys out because they were loners, which made them easy targets, but also because they had a similar build to him. When he came back, he shot them with a large-calibre bullet in the same place he'd struck them earlier, to cover up the evidence.

It all fits. The first time, here in Harlem, he arrived early with Russell Rod and led him into the closet. He hit him once, maybe more, on the back of the head with the butt of the gun, in exactly the spot where he'd later put a bullet through his brain. Then he went all the way downstairs, waiting for the place to fill up before heading back up on a trail of destruction. Once he'd done the job, he hid in the corner where I found him, shitting himself to make it look like he was terrified.'

Doris shook her head.

'Seems a bit much to me. Would a seventeen-year-old kid really do something that twisted?'

Lamar leant towards her.

'Don't forget he's been kicked out of school four times! He's a ... troubled character. He's been plotting his revenge for months, figuring out a way to get back at the schools until he came up with this screwed-up plan.'

Lamar glanced down at his watch.

'OK, we're good to go – D'Amato must be in position now.'

They walked up the front steps to the row of mail boxes. A label on one of them read 'DeRoy'. First-floor apartment.

They crept quietly up to the only door off the first-floor landing. Lamar pounded on the door before stepping aside. Doris positioned herself on the other side of the door frame.

A woman's voice called out from inside, 'Who is it?'

Doris signalled to Lamar that she would do the talking.

'Police, ma'am!' she replied. 'Open up right away.'

The door opened a crack, held back with a chain. A puffy face appeared in the opening. Doris held up her police badge, while Lamar kept his hand behind his back, ready to pull out his weapon if necessary.

'We need to talk to Chris urgently.'

The woman's round face creased with worry.

'What's he done?'

'Is he there, ma'am?' Doris pressed.

She shook her head.

'He went out twenty minutes ago.'

'He tell you where he was going?'

'No, that's not his style. He took a big bag with him, told me he wouldn't be back tonight.'

Lamar stepped in.

'Isn't he supposed to be recovering from his traumatic experience?'

The mother spat back, 'Sure, it shook him up! But he's allowed to leave the house, isn't he? He's gotta get some air sometimes, buck himself up.'

Lamar moved closer and looked the plump woman in the eye.

'Can I come in and take a look at his room?'

She was shaking with rage.

'No, no you cannot! This is my home!'

Lamar let it go, turning to Doris and taking her aside.

'Go tell D'Amato what's going on and get me a search warrant,' he told her. 'Explain everything to the judge, get him a copy of Chris DeRoy's school records and tell him to put a warning out to the mayor's office and the NYPD. We need to keep a watch on the two other schools before he strikes again.'

Doris nodded and hurried back downstairs.

Lamar turned back to the half-open door.

'I'm going to wait here until the warrant arrives,' he announced, pointing to the stairs.

The teenager's mother frowned, paused for a moment and then shut the door.

Ten minutes later, she flung the door wide open and stood there, dressed in a dirty tracksuit.

'You'd better come in then, since you will anyway when your damned piece of paper arrives.'

Lamar stood up and followed her into the apartment. It was a wreck, with wallpaper hanging off the walls. The only thing that had had any money spent on it was a large TV set, perched on a wobbly table in front of a worn-out sofa. An eighties soap was on with the sound turned off.

'His room's down the end of the hall. You can look, but don't touch anything. He'd give me hell if he knew.'

Lamar resisted telling her it was very unlikely her son would be coming back to lay into her. He walked down a dark corridor to reach a door covered in a Slayer poster.

The narrow room looked just like the rest of the apartment: filthy and messy. The duvet had been thrown on the floor, surrounded by music magazines and pirated CDs. Lamar scanned the room, stopping in front of an open closet. T-shirts had been pulled out and flung on the floor. Lamar knelt down to get a closer look at something shining at the bottom of the closet.

When he realised what it was, his heart started thumping.

He gulped.

They would have to expect the worst.

9

Several boxes were crammed in side by side. They had been emptied in a hurry, a few bullets left nestling among the clothes. Lamar picked up a 9mm cartridge.

Chris DeRoy had gone out carrying enough ammunition to shoot half of Harlem. How had he got hold of it all?

'Mrs DeRoy!' the detective called.

She skulked into the room.

'Yeah?'

'Were you aware that your son was keeping boxes full of bullets in his bedroom?'

She looked at him, as if hoping he would provide the answer.

'Well, er … I'm not surprised,' she finally admitted. 'He loves guns. He reads tons of books about them.'

Lamar looked around, shifting the magazines strewn over the floor with his foot.

'Can't see any here. Did he get them from a library?'

'Now that I couldn't tell you. You'd have to ask him. Why do you want to know, anyway? What's he been up to? Will you just tell me—'

'Does your son own any firearms?'

'How should I know?'

'You don't know if Christian has a gun?'

She was flustered.

'No … I mean, I know he's into that stuff, that's all. I don't think he has a gun, but I couldn't say for sure, with the kind of people he hangs out with …'

'What people?'

She waved her arms about.

'I don't know their names! But you can tell by looking at them they're no good.'

Lamar paused.

'Do you mean …' he began, 'they're black kids? Is that what you're saying?'

'No! Not at all. The opposite, actually. They're all white, and proud of it, you know? Some kind of militants, you might say. They don't come up here, but they sometimes hang out in the cellar downstairs.'

'There's a cellar here?'

'Oh, just a little one. Chris likes to go down there when he has people over.'

'Do you have the key?'

She scowled, before nodding.

'This way.'

She handed him two brown keys and told him how to get down there. Lamar went out of the building and found a door under the front steps, which he opened with the first key.

The steps quickly descended into darkness. Lamar fumbled about until he found the light switch. A bare bulb lit a long, damp corridor, with four padlocked doors leading off it. Lamar found the right one and walked closer, gripping his Walther P99. Though the air was cool below ground, Lamar could feel sweat dripping down his back.

The padlock was fastened. Christian DeRoy couldn't be inside.

The detective unlocked the door and walked into the musty cellar. He took the small torch out of his coat pocket and turned it on, sweeping its narrow beam over the gloom.

The first thing he saw was a pile of wooden crates, which had been used to make a table and stools. Candles had been left to melt down, spilling their wax over the table. There were stacks of back issues of gun-enthusiast magazines on the floor.

The beam picked out empty beer bottles and cigarette stubs.

Lamar bent his wrist to tilt the shaft of light upwards.

It flashed over a poster with the slogan 'Black and Hispanic scum out!'.

He had to step back to get a proper look at what he saw next. A huge flag hanging on the opposite wall.

An enormous blood-red banner. With a white circle in the middle. And a swastika turning at its centre.

10

Newton Capparel got out of his car and made a beeline for Lamar. It was dark at six o'clock and the glow of the streetlamps stained the snow, making it look as though the whole neighbourhood were covered in orange peel.

'I got your message,' he said. 'What's going on?'

The detective stood back to let D'Amato walk past carrying a box filled with items taken from Christian DeRoy's bedroom. A stream of people went in and out, searching the scene and sorting through anything of significance.

Lamar replied calmly, 'The three high-school massacres were a set-up. It's like I said on the phone: Chris DeRoy's our man in all three cases.'

'But he's just a kid.'

'Yes, but he's also an extremist. A fascist, a neo-Nazi. And I don't think he's alone either. Seems there's a whole bunch of them. I just hope he hasn't signed them all up for his next rampage.'

Capparel nodded towards the three detectives busily searching the apartment.

'Before you took the liberty of giving the order to search the premises, I'd have appreciated a call, Gallineo. And I would have warned you against it. We should have staked the place out and waited for the kid to come home, instead of taking over the whole neighbourhood. He'll turn and run the minute he sees all this!'

Lamar pointed to both ends of the road.

'Maddox and Rod are in position at either end of the street, keeping lookout. They've got photos of Christian. It's dark and, with all this snow, he isn't going to see us before we spot him.'

'So there's six of you here! Jeez. The two of us need to talk once we've wound this up. Instead of sending detectives out to waste their time, I'm going to have a photograph of this kid circulated to all the cops on patrol in the area. That'll be a damn sight more useful.'

With that, he turned on his heel and left before Lamar could respond, jumping into his car and driving off angrily.

This semi-success had not been Newton Capparel's idea, and Lamar could see it pissed him off.

He sighed and looked around for Doris. She had just loaded another crate into the van.

'Doris, I need your help again.'

'At your service, boss.'

He turned and gestured to the apartments looking onto the street.

'We need to talk to the neighbours. Teenagers, especially. Do they know Chris DeRoy? What can they tell us about him? And, most importantly, can they give us the names of anybody he hangs out with? Anybody at all.'

She nodded, looking a little downbeat.

'It'll be a lot of work.'

'Ask D'Amato to give you a hand. I think we're first in line this time.'

'What are you going to do? You must have some kind of plan if you're getting out of here.'

Lamar smiled.

'I'm going to sink into a white world,' he said, holding his hands out in front of him to catch the snow. 'A spotless universe for "the pure".'

Lamar headed back to base and sat down beside the phone, rubbing his hands together to warm them up. There were a few things he needed to check out.

His theory of a single killer in the shape of Chris DeRoy was looking more and more likely, but he needed to be sure he could apply it to all three attacks. As far as the Harlem high school was concerned, he was satisfied it all added up.

He took out the file on the Queens massacre.

The killer had worn a hood that covered his face, but several students thought they recognised him as one of their classmates by his distinctive clothes. Up to that point, it tallied with Harlem.

The gunman had fled after the attack. The police had identified him an hour later, based on the statements of a few witnesses who thought they recognised the denim jacket, plastered in heavy-metal badges. He'd 'committed suicide' with a bullet through the head.

So that was how Christian DeRoy had got close to his victim: they shared the same taste in music. The police would have to be careful not to generalise in order to avoid a media storm railing against the influence of goth culture and heavy-metal bands. Rap had been under the spotlight in the eighties, and the press always liked to find a new scapegoat, or at least tar a whole group of people with the same brush.

After the Queens shooting, Chris DeRoy had rushed back to his waiting victim, who probably lay unconscious. He had swapped the clothes back as usual, before killing him, making it look like suicide.

The third massacre had proceeded along the same lines before DeRoy had gone down into that underground room, where Mike Simmons was no doubt already in place.

Lamar remembered the door with the broken chain and padlock. A city worker had turned up later to explain it was a way down to the sewers, for maintenance. That was written in one of the reports Lamar had read. The padlock and chain had been sent off for analysis, but the results hadn't come back yet.

Lamar picked up the receiver and dialled the number of the Manhattan forensic unit. He was put through to two different people before eventually getting hold of Kathy Osbom. The pair had known each other for twelve years, having joined the NYPD at the same time.

It turned out Kathy knew all about the padlock and chain. Although her team wasn't involved in the investigation, she was following the case as it evolved. So far they had only tested for fingerprints, which hadn't revealed anything. The next stage would take some time, but Kathy didn't hold out much hope of uncovering vital clues.

Lamar asked her if it was possible for someone to have escaped through the exit, slipping their hand back round the door to pull the chain across behind them. Kathy had to admit she wasn't sure. It sounded plausible, but they would need to test the idea out to be certain.

Lamar thanked her, dialling the number for the FBI right after he'd hung up. He got straight through to one of his contacts at the Bureau, and was pleased to find him still at work at dinner time.

Lamar explained he needed to take a look at the Bureau's

reports on neo-Nazi activists in New York. He knew the FBI kept a close eye on these sorts of militants as part of the fight against terrorism, especially since the Timothy McVeigh case. For some time, the FBI had been criticised for focusing only on Islamist extremism, seeming to forget the threat posed by the far right, in spite of the damage it had already caused. The truth, as Lamar knew, was that the Bureau was still adding to its files on a regular basis.

The agent, Clark Fenton, agreed to send over everything he had as soon as he could, and urged Lamar to put a call out to all the precincts in New York since most of the FBI's intelligence came from police officers on the ground.

Lamar spent the next two hours trying to put out a request for information through his superiors at the NYPD. He was held back not by refusals but by the fact that most of them had gone home. It was almost nine.

The detective was polishing off a burrito when the fax machine started spitting out paper. It was a circular, instructing members of every precinct to contact Lamar Gallineo immediately should they have any recent intelligence on persons or groups suspected of involvement in neo-Nazi or similar activities, or of sharing such ideologies.

His computer let out a little beep, alerting him to a new email.

Clark Fenton had got back to him as promised.

'Synchronicity,' mumbled Lamar, opening the attachment.

Fenton had sent a summary of all known neo-Nazi activity in the city of New York and surrounding areas.

It named several small cells, but drew particular attention to two larger groups, described as 'alarming'.

Lamar read through the document, making the occasional note but not convinced any of it was of much use to him.

Three of the smaller clusters were predominantly made up of teenagers, who had usually been manipulated, or 'recruited'. Two of these operated out of Manhattan: one from the Alphabet City area to the south, the other from the Upper West Side. The first group met in its members' apartments, but hadn't actually committed any recorded acts. They used their meetings to exchange opinions and strengthen each other's views, according to the report's writer. The second group was harder to pin down; they'd been seen in Central Park after dark and in several disused subway stations, most often the one on 91st Street.

All of them were suspected of trafficking of one sort or another, usually drugs, on a fairly small scale and without much organisation. Occasionally they ventured into firearms, which the report judged to be 'a more serious issue'.

Lamar leant back in his seat.

Another cop by the name of Arnold was sitting at his desk on the other side of the room, head down, putting together a report.

Lamar rubbed his face slowly, as his ideas crystallised and became more conclusive.

Chris DeRoy often had his 'friends' over to the cellar at his place. That suggested they didn't live far from him. Whether coming from Alphabet City or the Upper West Side, it was a short bus or subway ride to Harlem.

But a trainee fascist living in Harlem? Pretty ironic, given that the neighbourhood had such a strong black identity. No doubt it was his parents, and not him, who had chosen the area.

Lamar looked over at Doris's empty chair. She hadn't come back. It was a hell of a lot of work getting statements from all the neighbours and you often had to wait until people came home in the evening to be able to question them all.

The detective checked his watch: nine thirty. Doris would probably be back at her apartment by now, snuggled up watching the wrestling.

There was a noise behind him. As he turned round to see what it was, he caught a glimpse of Newton Capparel charging past. Lamar rushed over to the doorway and saw Capparel hurtling down the stairs.

'What's up?' Lamar called after him.

Newton glanced up at him.

'An officer on patrol spoke to a guy in a grocery store. He says he saw Christian DeRoy late this afternoon, not far from his apartment.'

'Is he absolutely sure it was him?'

'He recognised the kid as soon as he saw the photo!' Capparel gloated.

It had been his idea to send out patrols with pictures of the suspect. If the tactic led to DeRoy's arrest, he'd get all the glory, and all the time Lamar had spent raking through the details would be forgotten.

Capparel sprinted off again and was almost out of sight when Lamar leant over the handrail and called down to him, 'What was he doing at the store?'

Capparel waved away the question without looking up.

'Oh, buying candles or something.'

Lamar froze. Candles. A hint of a smile played across his lips.

It might be nothing, but he had to check it out for himself. With Christian DeRoy carrying enough weapons to wage a war, he couldn't afford to wait and see.

Doris walked in less than forty minutes later, certain of finding her colleague at his desk even at this late hour. Lamar would sleep in the office if he was working on a particularly pressing case.

She wanted to give him the news herself, face to face. She knew he would leap on it when he heard. But he was nowhere to be seen, and his stuff had gone too.

She noticed Arnold working in his corner and went over.

'You seen Lamar lately?'

Arnold nodded.

'He left less than an hour ago. Looked like he was in a hurry.'

'Know where he went?'

'No. Do you need him for something?'

Doris put her hands on her hips.

'Yeah, I do. The kid's mom talked. She told me her son got a call right before he rushed out.'

Arnold stared vacantly back at her. She carried on, for her own benefit.

'I've just found out where the call was made from.'

Arnold could see now she wasn't just rambling, but had something on her mind that she desperately needed to share.

'It came from a telephone in the hall at East Harlem Academy. Just after Lamar left there this afternoon.'

11

A cold wind was blowing through the arteries at the heart of Manhattan.

The snow was falling softly now, just a few scattered flakes, but a thick layer covered the ground, making the roads and pavements look higher than they were.

Lamar's ear was glued to his cell phone: the invention of the century for the police.

He kept being passed from one person to the next at MTA, the New York transit authority, before getting hold of the direct line for one of the managers, who told him how to get to the abandoned subway station on 91st Street and assured him someone would meet him there with the keys.

Lamar's reasoning was very simple.

If Chris DeRoy had been spotted buying candles after leaving his place, there was a chance he might belong to the cluster which met in the disused subway station. If it turned out he was barking up entirely the wrong tree, he'd only have wasted his own time, and at least he could rule out a line of inquiry.

After parking the car, Lamar walked to the corner of Amsterdam Avenue and 91st Street, where a man in an MTA uniform was waiting for him, his hands in his pockets. Lamar introduced himself. The subway worker, Carl, had a small moustache and was carrying a few extra pounds.

Carl led the way to a building, unlocked a heavy door and started down the stairs. Within a few seconds, they had left the icy gusts of air outside for the sheltered maze of the abandoned station.

'The reports I've read say kids come down here a lot,' began Lamar, 'but how do they get in? I'm guessing they don't have their own keys.'

'Oh, there's no shortage of ways in. The old entrances have been blocked up but kids break through them all the time. It's like a block of Swiss cheese down here, with ways in and out all over the place, leading to the sewers, underpasses and even the cellars underneath some buildings. But, you know, I sometimes think to myself maybe we should be thankful they're messing around down here, out of everyone's way!'

Carl sniggered to himself.

They walked quickly down the concrete steps, with only Carl's Maglite torch to light the way. The walls were plastered in colourful graffiti. Empty alcohol and soda bottles littered the ground, like apocalyptic flora growing from the bunker's soil.

'Don't you worry, we can get a light on in just a minute!' Carl cheerfully announced.

'I'd rather we didn't. It might scare off the guy I'm looking for.'

Carl stopped in his tracks and cleared his throat.

'Oh, so you're here to arrest somebody? OK, I, er …'

Sensing his unease, Lamar pre-empted him.

'How about you head back up, Carl? I'll meet you where we came in. Don't worry, I'll find my way.'

Carl agreed instantly.

'O-o-h, and … um …' stuttered Lamar, 'call this number if I'm not back within the hour.'

He handed Carl one of Doris's business cards, which he carried with him at all times.

Carl swapped his powerful flashlight for Lamar's little torch and scurried up the steps.

Left alone, the detective took his cell phone from his pocket to check for a signal. Nothing. Now he really was on his own.

He carried on down a dank, dirty corridor that stank of urine until he came to one last stairway down. As he put his foot on the first step something glinted in the torchlight.

Lamar was forced to stretch out his leg to avoid hitting the obstacle in his way. The sole of his shoe skidded on the step and he flailed his arms about to try to restore his balance. He swung round, eventually finding his footing again, his legs four steps apart. He shone the light closer to see what had almost tripped him up.

It was a long row of empty glass bottles, lined up perfectly.

Lamar could see he had narrowly avoided stepping into a trap. Or, rather, a warning sign. If somebody came down the stairs, they were very likely to knock over the bottles, sending them toppling noisily down. *I must be getting close*.

He took his gun out of its holster and forced himself to go on.

Finally he reached the platform. A succession of graffiti-scrawled pillars lay between him and the shadowy passageways leading off to the left and right. He kept close to the wall, sweeping his torch over the darkness to try to pick out a figure, or at least something to indicate someone had been here not long before.

An amber glow emerged from one of the tunnels, where subway trains had once rattled by. Lamar edged closer, treading as softly as he could. He turned off his torch in order not to be seen, creeping forward almost on tiptoe.

He reached the end of the platform and slowly heaved himself down onto the tracks. The light was flickering less than thirty feet away from him.

Candlelight ...

Lamar raised his gun. He knew it was against procedure – he could shoot accidentally if startled or overcome with nerves. But it was a risk he was willing to take. Better that than the first bullet finding him.

Eventually an alcove came into view, where a few candles were burning on the ground. A figure huddled in a blanket sat with his back against the wall, holding a bottle in his hand.

Just a tramp. Lamar eased back, lowering his Walther P99.

Then he saw the fingers. Quite slender, more or less clean, with no signs of age. The hand of a teenager.

Lamar stayed primed.

The shape on the floor seemed to have caught sight of the detective, lifting his head and letting the blanket slip off his shoulders.

Chris DeRoy's dark pupils stared straight into Lamar's eyes. The mask of the traumatised kid had fallen. Now his features were contorted by hate as his true nature was revealed.

12

Lamar aimed his gun at the young man.

'Don't move!' he barked. 'It's over, Chris. It's over.'

Christian DeRoy clenched his jaw, his face tensing with rage.

'No son of a bitch nigger's gonna tell me when it's over,' he spat back.

Something moved quickly under the blanket at chest level.

Lamar roared, 'NO!'

Raw fear swept aside any hesitation. Lamar's finger pressed down hard on the trigger.

The gun bellowed, spraying out hot steel.

The blanket lifted as a burst of dark liquid came spurting out of Christian DeRoy's chest. The boy started shaking and fell sideways into the grit.

Lamar rushed over to him. A revolver appeared from under the blanket. Chris DeRoy held it limply, his eyes rolling.

The gun fired twice in Lamar's general direction. The bullets disappeared into the eternal darkness of the tunnel.

Lamar grabbed hold of Chris's hand, breaking several of his fingers with a loud crack. He kicked the revolver away before kneeling down beside the injured boy.

The shaking had turned into powerful convulsions.

Chris lifted his head to look at Lamar. He opened his mouth, twisted in pain and hate. He was trying to say something.

'Don't … touch …'

Blood trickled down his chin. Lamar couldn't make out the rest of what he said.

The lieutenant lifted up the boy's sweater and ripped open his shirt to look at the wound. Right in the middle of the chest. Whether through the lungs or the heart, Lamar couldn't say.

Chris DeRoy's legs jolted, knocking over a candle and putting out another. Suddenly the light became very dim. The flame of the candle rolling on its side went out.

Lamar could feel warm blood trickling down his hands as he knelt in the shadows.

The teenager's breathing was fast and shallow. Then it stopped. Silence. Christian DeRoy let out a long rattle and then he too was snuffed out.

After a minute or so Lamar stood up and turned on his torch. He needed to get back up to the surface and let everyone know what had happened.

He stepped away, trying not to think about what he had just done. Killed a teenager.

On legitimate grounds of self defence.

Still meant he'd killed the kid.

He heard the sound of running footsteps crunching through the gravel towards him. Lamar pointed the torch in that direction. A man threw his arms up in front of his face to shield his eyes from the glare.

Lamar recognised the build, the crumpled suit. The figure slowly brought his arms down.

It was Allistair McLogan, the principal at East Harlem Academy.

'McLogan?' Lamar choked in shock.

'Is that you, Lieutenant?'

'What are you doing here?'

McLogan came closer.

'What am I doing here?' he echoed. 'I've come to help one of my students, whether you like it or not!'

Lamar was baffled. He put away his gun and stepped towards the principal.

'What's that supposed to mean?'

McLogan drew level with him.

'Chris told me everything. He called me an hour ago. You're one nasty piece of work, Lieutenant, and racist too by the sounds of it! Picked on him because he's a white kid, did you?'

Lamar shook his head.

'You've lost me. He told you everything about what?'

'Don't play the fool with me!' bellowed McLogan, pointing his finger at Lamar. 'He told me you've been hounding him. You singled him out; you were determined to make things difficult for him. He was so scared of you and what you might do he ran away and came here, absolutely terrified. So he turned to me and asked me to come and talk to him, calm him down and take him back home.'

Lamar held his hand up to stop McLogan coming any closer.

'Now wait a second, you've got this all—'

'Your methods are totally unacceptable, Lieutenant! You—'

McLogan stopped, catching sight of the blood on Lamar's hands.

'What have you done?'

He scanned all around him, straining to see in the darkness. Suddenly he froze.

'So that's what I heard? Not firecrackers then, huh? It was gunfire? You ... you shot him?' McLogan asked, his disbelief quickly turning to outrage.

Lamar was about to protest when alarm bells started to ring. McLogan was here on the pretext that Chris had asked him to come. Doing everything he could to protect the boy. Could it be ... An adult in a position of influence, who might well know how to manipulate a kid.

But just as these doubts began to form McLogan's brains exploded from the shadows, spattering over Lamar's chest and face as a deafening shot rang out in the tunnel.

A fourth person was walking towards them.

13

A shape emerged in the circle of light cast by Lamar's torch.

A pistol was pointing at him.

Lamar recognised the close-cropped hair and the round face: Frank Quincey, grinning.

'One down!' shouted the janitor of the school where it had all started. 'Never could stand the jerk.'

'Calm down, Quincey. Put down weapon away.'

He laughed.

'Who do you think you are?' he challenged Lamar. 'Who are you to be giving orders to anybody? No, I will not put down my goddamn gun. And you know what? I'm going to kill you.'

Lamar tried to breathe calmly and get a handle on the situation. If he gave in to fear, all would be lost. He had to buy himself some time, find a way out of this. He had to talk to Quincey. Make *him* talk.

'Quincey,' he began, 'why ... why are you doing this?'

'*Why?* Jeez, you really are one dumb black fucker, aren't you? Well, luckily for our future civilisation there are people like me around. And people like these kids, just waiting to be told what to do. Like Christian. Good kid, that one. Smart. Didn't take long for him to get it. When I saw the way he looked at all the Puerto Ricans and Mexicans, I knew we were thinking the same thing. We both knew how to make the world a better place. After that, the little guy didn't come to see me just to bum cigarettes!'

Quincey was getting himself worked up, his eyes sparkling with excitement.

'I brought him into our group, the next generation. Kids I found on the streets, kids forgotten by our corrupt system! The little guy soon stepped up to take part in our eradication project. All I had to do was get him the weapons.'

Lamar racked his brains for some way out of the dead end he found himself trapped in. He ran over every possible escape route. Meanwhile, Quincey's impassioned soliloquy was in full swing.

'Imagine, Detective, a world in which teenagers started shooting down their schoolmates, not just aiming at coloured scum, but the whole damn lot of them! They're all tainted, the liars and cheats of tomorrow! What Christian did was to set an example. Soon others will do the same and then all hell will break loose. There'll be armies of young people, and the police will be too scared to fire on them. We're going to turn this country upside down, and then we're going to make it right again!'

Quincey lifted his arm until the gun was pointing right at Lamar's head.

'And, in our new order, you'll go back to being a slave. You were born subhuman and that's what you'll always be.'

Lamar gripped the torch in his hand, running his forefinger over the top of it.

'Well, I say "you",' Quincey continued, 'what I should have said is "your kind". Because you're bowing out tonight, mister.'

The light shook a little while Lamar turned the heavy torch in his hand.

'You see, history doesn't always repeat itself!' Quincey said with a wry smile. 'Sometimes the fascists win. And as for you, nigger, time's up.'

Finally Lamar's fingertips found what they'd been searching for. The on/off switch on his torch. Quincey was taking aim, his finger poised to pull the trigger.

Lamar flicked the switch. They were suddenly in total darkness. Lamar leapt down from the platform just as a shot whistled by a few inches from his head.

He rolled on the track and tried to scramble back to his feet to avoid losing his bearings completely. He steadied himself on his knees and took out his Walther P99.

Quincey was pacing around, searching, breathing heavily. He stumbled into something, probably Christian DeRoy's body, and fired. Again and again.

Some of the bullets left no trace as they were fired; others left a flaming trail in their wake. Lamar aimed at the flashes of light and fired all his remaining bullets.

When Lamar turned his torch back on after ten minutes of uneasy silence, he saw Frank Quincey's body slumped over the corpse of his seventeen-year-old disciple. Their blood mingled together deep beneath the city.

Quincey twitched. He wasn't dead.

Lamar bolted towards him, loading another round of bullets. He held the hot barrel against the fascist's head. Did he deserve to live after everything he had done?

The rumble of a far-off subway train travelled through the bowels of the earth. Down here, away from civilised society, away from judgement and conscience, Lamar had a choice.

He breathed in deeply, to gather his courage. Hate was flowing the other way now.

Epilogue

Lamar Gallineo was suspended for three weeks.

During that time, Internal Affairs conducted an investigation to corroborate Lieutenant Gallineo's statements. The report found he had acted on legitimate grounds of self defence when he had opened fire on Christian DeRoy and Frank Quincey.

He had played no part in the death of the school principal and had done nothing to put Allistair McLogan's life in danger. Frank Quincey and Christian DeRoy alone were responsible.

After Lamar had left the Harlem high school that day, Quincey had called his protégé to warn him that the police were looking for him. Chris DeRoy had fled to their hideout. Later that evening, the young man had called the principal at home to lure him into a trap and eliminate him. They all deserved to die in his eyes, by whatever means.

After his suspension Gallineo went back to work, where his colleagues showered him with messages of support. He returned to his desk opposite Doris, who had visited him at home while he was off. Everything was getting back to normal.

But it was a long time before he could look at a high school again without thinking of all the vulnerable teenagers inside and how easily they could be led. Some were hard as rock, but others could be moulded like balls of clay.

The streets of New York were no less safe than the other big cities of the world. But you could never rely on reason to stand firm. Every day, men and women threatened to tip the fragile balance holding up civil society.

Lamar had no sympathy for them. They may have been hurt, may have had troubled childhoods, but the fact remained that at every step of the way they had, and still had, a choice. Just as he'd had.

The trial of Frank Quincey took place in Manhattan, in a state which administered the death penalty. He was sentenced to death. When the verdict was announced, he stood up and made a fascist salute.

As the prison guards led him to Execution Chamber Five years later, at 4.30 a.m. on 18 December, he crumbled. He cried. Begged for forgiveness. Pleaded to be given another chance. Swore he wouldn't let them down.

Entering the room where he would breathe his last, he

fell to his knees. He wet himself. It took four guards to strap him to the chair. It was silent, but for his whimpering.

It took seventeen minutes to kill him, according to the doctor who examined him to ensure his heart had stopped.

The room was cleaned immediately afterwards, left immaculate for the break of a new day.

Spotless, anonymous, waiting for the next one.

Basic
Organic
Chemistry